R(Moves In

Story by Pamela Rushby

Illustrations by Paul Könye

Contents

Chapter 1

The Rules

"No ball games in the apartment grounds!"
someone shouted. "You know the rules!"

Grace, Lee, Ahmed and Jack
stopped kicking Ahmed's soccer ball
and turned around.
They knew who was shouting.
It was Mr William Grimm,
the caretaker of their apartment building.

Mr Grimm ran up
and put his foot on Ahmed's ball.
"What are the rules?" he said sternly.

The children sighed.
"No ball games," said Grace.

"No bikes," said Lee.

"No rollerblades," said Jack.

"And especially no pets," said Ahmed.

"Good, you know the rules.
Now, get off to the park and play there,"
said Mr Grimm.

The children had been on their way to the park.
It was right behind their building.
They'd only kicked the ball a few times.
But Mr Grimm's apartment was on the ground floor,
right by the front door. He saw everything.

Chapter 2

At the Park

"I get the first kick!" Grace said, when they got to the park.

"Why you?" Jack said. "It's Ahmed's ball!"

"It's all right, I don't mind," Ahmed said. He liked everyone to be happy.

Grace put the ball on the ground and kicked it as hard as she could.

"Huh!" Jack said. "Great kick! It went straight into the bushes!"

Grace pulled a face and ran to get the ball.
She reached into the bushes.
Then she jumped back.
"There's something moving in there!" she cried.

The boys ran up.
Grace pushed the bushes aside and peered in.

"Be careful!" said Lee.
"You don't know what it is!"

"It's all right," Grace said softly. "It's a parrot.
And I think it's hurt its wing."

The parrot was beautiful.
It was red and blue and green and yellow.
It looked up at them with bright black eyes.
One wing was trailing on the ground.

"What do you do with an injured parrot?"
asked Ahmed.

"You take it to the vet!" said Jack.
"There's one just down the street."

"But we have to catch it first," said Lee.
"It might bite!"

"I know what to do," Ahmed said.
He pulled off his jacket
and dropped it gently over the parrot.
Then he held the parrot carefully
and rolled it in his jacket.
The parrot was very quiet
as they walked to the vet.

Chapter 3

No Pets!

Dr Ford, the vet,
thought that the parrot was someone's pet.
"It's very tame," she said.
"I wouldn't be surprised if it could talk."

The parrot looked at her.
"Cup of tea?" it said. "Cup of tea? Bill?"

Dr Ford laughed. "There you are!
It wants a cup of tea and the bill!
Now, let's look at that wing."

Dr Ford said that the wing wasn't broken.
She thought it would be better in about ten days.
"I'll put up a notice to try to find the owner,"
she said.
"But it really needs some special looking after.
If I lend you a cage and tell you what to do,
could you take it home
and look after it until it's better?"

The children looked at each other.
A parrot was a pet.
And the rules said – no pets!

"If we could get it past Mr Grimm,
we could take turns looking after it until it's better," Lee said.

"But Mr Grimm sees everything
that goes in and out!" Grace said.

"I've got an idea!" Ahmed said.
"I'll be back in a few minutes!"

No Pets!

19

Chapter 4

Babysitting Rosie

When Ahmed came back,
he was pushing his baby sister's pram.

"A pram?" everyone said.

"If we cover the cage with my sister's blanket,
Mr Grimm won't see it," Ahmed explained.

"Great idea!" Grace said, picking up the cage.
"Come on, Rosie, in you go!"

"Rosie?" said Jack.
"Who said it's called Rosie?"

"I did," Grace said.
"Do you have any problems with that?"

Jack thought about it. "I guess not," he said.

Mr Grimm was near the front door
as Ahmed pushed the pram
into the apartment building.

"So, what are you lot up to now?" he said.

"Nothing," said Lee.

22

"Not a thing," said Jack.

"We're just looking after Rosie," said Grace.

"Babysitting, are you?" said Mr Grimm.
"Well, that should keep you out of trouble!"

The children looked at each other.
Mr Grimm had no idea how wrong he was!

Ahmed pushed the pram through the door.

And Rosie was in!